SAMURAI

Book # 6 in the TIME SOLDIERS® Series

By KATHLEEN DUEY

Created & Photographed by
ROBERT GOULD

Digital Illustration & 3D Special Effects by
EUGENE EPSTEIN

One rainy morning, six neighborhood kids find a time portal in the woods. Through swirling green light, they can see a living dinosaur! They can't convince their parents the portal exists, so they pack their camping gear and go through it, armed with a videocamera. They outrun Velociraptors, and outwit a T-Rex—and make it home with an incredible videotape.

PATCH

GREEN STONE

TIME PORTAL ENTRANCE

REX

But before they can show it to anyone, a mysterious man in a dark suit and sunglasses steals it.
The portal opens the very next day. Then nearly a year goes by before it transports them back in time again. Dinosaurs, pirates, knights, a boy pharaoh in ancient Egypt: With every adventure, the Time Soldiers learn more about history, about themselves, and about a timeless secret.

Robert Gould's
TIME SOLDIERS

The Ultimate Adventure Series

Book # 6
SAMURAI

by **Kathleen Duey**

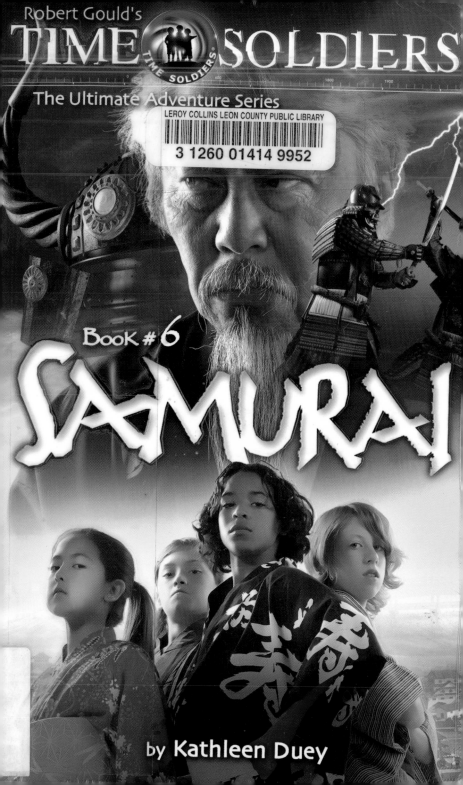

TIME SOLDIERS®
Book # 6 SAMURAI

Text © 2006 Kathleen Duey
Photography © 2006 Robert Gould
Digital Illustrations © 2006 Eugene Epstein

Library of Congress Control Number: 2005935054
ISBN: 1-929945-63-9

Reading is more fun with

BiG GUY BOOKS Inc.

www.bigguybooks.com

Published by BiG GUY BOOKS, Inc.
6359 Paseo Del Lago • Suite B
Carlsbad, CA 92011 USA

Printed in USA

Check out all the NEW STUFF at www.bigguybooks.com

Brian has made a tough decision. He's been accepted into special classes that will qualify him for a scholarship. Since he has to study so much, the Time Soldiers are looking for someone to replace him. They are all working to stay fit, research times and places they want to explore, and learn survival skills while they decide where to go next.

ARTHUR

AMULET

MUMMY

The men in dark suits are watching the Time Soldiers very closely. They know why the four oldest kids—Jon, Adam, Rob and Mariah—can't go through the portal anymore. They know about the strange green stones. And they know that time is running out… .

The library was quiet. "I can't decide," Luke was saying. "I want to go a hundred places." He noticed a girl sitting nearby and gestured. "She's here every time we come."

Mikey turned to look. The girl was lost in the book she was reading. "Maybe we should talk to her. We need someone smart."

"She's good at martial arts, too," Bernardo said.
"I've seen her practicing at the dojo."
   Luke leaned forward. "We should find out more about her."

Everyone liked Nami and they talked to her more each day. Finally, they decided to ask her to become a Time Soldier. She looked amazed—and excited.

"Could we go to Edo, the city that became Tokyo?" Nami asked, "I speak Japanese and I have samurai ancestors."

"Samurai?" Mikey asked. Bernardo and Luke smiled.

Two men in dark suits and mirrored sunglasses stared at the organic diode screen. The picture was perfect. "Should we get the stone now?" one asked.

The other frowned. "Why? They will find more pieces of it and—"

"Or they could lose it," the first man said.

"We're all getting better," Bernardo said after class. "Our research is nearly done. We're almost ready."

"The Samurai fascinate me," Nami said. "They were always trying to serve, to protect. But I'm a little afraid," she added. "You've done this before, but I can barely believe it's true."

"Everyone is a little scared," Mikey said, then he smiled. "We always stick together and we get home safe. And this time, you'll be able to translate for us."

Nami nodded. "I can't wait."

"These costumes are incredible!" Mikey said. "Are you sure your father won't mind?"

Nami smiled. "As long as we take care of everything, no one will even notice. I checked my father's production schedules. They won't need these for a year or more."

Luke nodded. "We had to borrow grave clothes in Egypt. We put them back, but it felt wrong to use them at all. This is going to be so much easier!"

Bernardo laughed. "In medieval England, we actually sewed our camp blankets into robes."

On a sunny Saturday morning, the Time Soldiers changed into their costumes and hiked into the woods. Bernardo held the amulet tightly. He focused his thoughts the way Brian had taught him and

Luke pointed. "I think I see a path that leads in the right direction."

They walked through the forest for hours before

The Time Soldiers walked closer. "Look," Luke whispered, "a samurai teacher and his students!" Bernardo took a deep breath. "I managed to get us close to the city, but did I miss the time target?"

Mikey shook his head. "No, look at the clothes and the style of swords—we're in the era we studied, around 1700AD."

They all fell silent and watched the samurai working with his class.

The Time Soldiers hid and watched the classes until the sun was low in the sky. Then the samurai teacher started down the path, walking quickly, as though hours of training and teaching had not tired him at all.

"We should follow him," Mikey said. "He must know the best way into the city."

The Time Soldiers went just fast enough to glimpse the old man now and then. The plum blossoms made the air sweet. "It's so beautiful," Nami said. "I understand why the people here love nature so much."

An hour passed. Then two. "Did the teacher turn off somewhere?" Bernardo asked.

A moment later, the samurai leapt onto the path, his sword raised. Startled, Bernardo gripped the amulet as Nami began talking to the samurai in Japanese. Her voice was shaky, but the samurai listened. He lowered his sword, then sheathed it.

He spoke, then waited as Nami translated.

"I explained that we only followed him to find the city. He says if we camp with him, he'll show us the way in the morning."

"Taro No Yoshiie," the samurai said.

"That's his name," Nami said. "Bow in respect."

At sunset, the samurai made a campfire and shared his rice and meat. After they had eaten, he asked Nami where they lived. "Far from here," she answered in Japanese. "We came to learn about the samurai."

The old man raised his chin. "Samurai live in peace now. But when I was young, I was in many battles. One was in that clearing." He pointed. Nami translated.

"Would he tell us about it?" Bernardo whispered.

Nami spoke to the old man. He began to talk in a low voice.

The old man's voice was deep and strong. Nami translated.

"When I was young," he said, "I fought to defend my daimyo, my home and my ruler. I served him. I obeyed his orders. It was a hard life, but a proud one. He gave me a helmet for serving well."

about losing the helmet. He had been hurt—and he hadn't seen the thief—but someone had stolen the helmet. Another samurai? The old man shook his head. It seemed impossible.

The sunrise woke them all. The samurai led them to a tower, talking to Nami as they walked.

"This is so cool," Luke said as they stood, looking out over the battlefield.

"That's where he lost the helmet," Nami said, pointing.

After a moment, the samurai began to speak again. "He's talking about the battle now," Nami said quietly. "And he thanks us for listening to his old tales." She paused. "He says he would be honored to have us in his home."

As they followed the old man into Edo, he was talking to Nami. She kept turning back to translate. The samurai explained that the ancient city had begun as a single daimyo. Then other rulers had moved their families and farms closer to the sea. He was proud of his home. In Edo there were candles, he told them, that burned

The old man smiled, then spoke. "He wants to take us through the city now," Nami translated, "before most people are awake." They all knew that the samurai was protecting them and they

The samurai led them through shops and businesses. Then he followed one of the canals, walking toward the harbor so they could see the fishing boats. The Time Soldiers kept glancing at each other. It was strange to think

that one day this city would be modern Tokyo,
full of skyscrapers and cars. When the sun was
low in the afternoon sky, the samurai finally led
them back to his house.

The old man showed them his gardens. "Some of the bonsai trees are more than 200 years old," Nami said. "His ancestors cared for them."

The samurai's servants prepared food while he talked about the importance of honor. "He's teaching us like we're his students," Mikey whispered. Nami translated and the old man smiled.

In an instant, they were back on the battlefield—and fifty years back in time. The dark of night had vanished. It was a bright morning now and storm clouds were rolling in from the sea.

The two men were staring at their screens.
One of them rubbed his forehead. "We never had adventures like this."
The other man shrugged. "We didn't have time."
There was silence as they both tried not to laugh at the pun. It was true. They had been on assignment and their orders had been very clear.

"I wish we could just leave them alone," the first man said.

The second man didn't bother to answer him. It was impossible and they both knew it. Their orders had not changed.

The sounds of the battle were close, too close.
"This way!" Mikey shouted. They ran, then hid
near the place the samurai had pointed out—the
edge of the meadow where he had lost the helmet.
The Time Soldiers were still and silent, watching
the men fight. It was like they had fallen into an

action movie, but this was real. The warriors were galloping toward their enemies. The archers drew back their bows to take aim... .

"Where is he?" Nami asked over the pounding of the hooves and the shouts of battle.

Then she pointed. "I see him! There he is!"

"He's been hit!" Mikey yelled.

The daimyo had given it to the samurai to honor his courage and loyalty—and this ninja had stolen it!

Luke stood and faced the man. The fire from one of the towers had spread—he could feel the heat of the flames. The ninja stared at him, then turned and ran, fading into the smoke. Luke sprinted back to his friends. They were all talking fast, trying to come up with a plan.

"We can't follow a ninja!" Nami was saying. "We'll never manage to keep up. We can't see where he goes and—"

"We can from up there," Luke shouted, pointing at the only tower still standing. An instant later they were all running up the hill.

There was a second path, narrow and steep. They followed it downhill. Mikey and Bernardo silently climbed the steps of the little house to make sure the ninja was inside.

"Now what?" Nami whispered when they came back.

"I brought walkie-talkies," Luke said. "And Mikey

"Look," Mikey said. "The ninja's slowing down—he's turning into the forest."

"Spot a landmark," Bernardo said.

Mikey stared. "There's a crooked pine where he turned off. Let's go."

There was a second path, narrow and steep. They followed it downhill. Mikey and Bernardo silently climbed the steps of the little house to make sure the ninja was inside.

"Now what?" Nami whispered when they came back.

"I brought walkie-talkies," Luke said. "And Mikey

"We can't follow a ninja!" Nami was saying. "We'll never manage to keep up. We can't see where he goes and—"

"We can from up there," Luke shouted, pointing at the only tower still standing. An instant later they were all running up the hill.

"Can you see him?" Bernardo asked.

"No," Mikey said. "Wait. There he is, running down the path toward Edo."

Luke frowned. "I really wanted to give that helmet back to the samurai."

Bernardo hit the railing. "Me, too."

has stink bombs."

Bernardo reached into the belt pack he wore beneath his kimono. "Two laser pointers, fully charged." Nami was staring at them.

Mikey turned. "We all bring something in case of an emergency. We usually have at least one."

Five minutes later, they had a plan and Mikey had
climbed a tree. "Are the lasers bright enough?" he
heard Luke ask.

"I think so," Bernardo said. "And it's getting darker."

"Stink bombs work day or night," Mikey joked.

Nami stared up at him. "Aren't you afraid?"

"Sure," he told her as he secured the walkie-talkie.

"We were afraid of the evil knight and the Egyptian temple guards, too." He climbed down. "If everything goes well, we'll be fifty years away from here in a few minutes."

Bernardo glanced at Nami. She looked a little scared, but she seemed steady—she was holding the walkie-talkie firmly in one hand. Good. They had known she was smart and brave and she was proving it. "Everybody ready?" he asked quietly. "I am," Nami said.

The ninja made a noise inside the little house and Luke jumped, startled. They were all tense. Mikey nodded sharply. "Let's go."

unidentified
radio transmitter

digital rendering in proc

zone 07

The men in dark suits were staring at the simulscreens.
"I can't believe this," the first man said.
The second man was silent, then he exhaled. "They aren't bringing the stone back are they?"
The first man didn't answer. They both knew the truth. These kids were caught up in a thrilling adventure. Of course they would return the helmet

dragon appeared on the ninja's shoulder, flickered to the wall, then jumped back. The man turned, startled and confused. Bernardo shone the light at the far wall again. "It's working," he whispered to Nami.

Bernardo shifted his position. He shone the dragon-light against the window frame, then aimed it toward the door. The ninja turned to stare at it, then he took a step toward it. Bernardo nodded at Nami, then clicked the laser off. An instant later her voice, low and growling, came through the walkie-talkie Mikey had hung in the tree in front of the house. Nami sounded cold and stern as she pretended to be the dragon. She was challenging the ninja to a battle. Nami kept her voice low and fierce. "Come out and face us!" she said. "I dare you!"

The ninja stepped outside. Bernardo moved, turning on the second laser. He aimed the lights at the wooden porch beams. Nami knew the ninja had never seen a laser pointer and he had no idea what a walkie-talkie was. To him, the dragon's voice seemed real. "Can you catch us?" Nami snarled. "Do you dare to try?"

She signaled to Bernardo and he moved the light-dragons from the porch to tree trunks in front of the house.

For a long moment, the ninja followed the light-dragons with his eyes. Then, without warning, he leapt to the ground, his hands raised, ready to fight.

The ninja was still trying to catch the light-dragon. Nami glanced at Bernardo and wrinkled her nose. He nodded. He could smell it, too. Mikey had set off the stinkbombs.

Bernardo moved the light-dragons lower, letting the ninja come closer to them. Then, at the last second, he moved the images to the next tree— and the next—leading the ninja farther from the house, farther from the path. Bernardo glanced back and saw his friends heading uphill. It was time to go. For a few seconds more, Bernardo

Then the portal opened in front of them and they sprinted through it. Coming out into the darkness and silence of the samurai's garden, they all glanced back at the forest on the other side of the swirling green light.

"Can he follow us?" Nami shouted.

"Older kids can't go through without terrible pain," Mikey told her. "We're pretty sure adults can't do it at all."

Bernardo stared at the ninja shoving at the portal. "It almost looks like it's closing in order to stop him."

They all watched as the portal shrank and dimmed, then disappeared, keeping the ninja back in his own time.

"Taro No Yoshiie is going to be so happy to see this," Luke said, holding up the helmet.

"Look at the stone," Mikey said. "It looks like—"

"The stone in the amulet," Bernardo interrupted. "How can that be? Is it a coincidence?"

Luke wiped the dust of battle from the stone.

Suddenly, green light snaked between the stones. The helmet dragged Luke forward. He fought to hold on. Mikey helped him and they finally pulled it free, breaking the arc of light. "We need to do some research," Luke said. "Is there a green stone with magnetic properties?"

"One that can also open time portals?"
Bernardo added, shaking his head. He put the
amulet back in his pocket—the stone felt hot.
"Let's go inside," Nami said.

Taro No Yoshiie's eyes went wide when he saw the helmet. "Tell him we wanted to thank him," Mikey said. "We wanted to show our respect and esteem." Nami translated as the samurai took the helmet. His eyes were full of happiness. A few minutes later, he left the room, then came back carrying a beautifully carved box.

"He says it is for us to keep our treasures in,"
Nami told the others.

The Time Soldiers bowed one last time and
said goodbye, then walked a little ways into the
woods to open the portal and go home.

"A box?" the first man asked. "Carved and lacquered and—oh no!" As he spoke, the image flickered, then went dark. "They aren't bringing the second stone back, and now they have a box that shields the first one?"

to a riding school this summer. And we'll need to pick a time and place and—"

"Whoa," Luke said, and they all laughed.

To be continued...

CREDITS

Time Soldiers

Luke - Isiah Jackson
Mikey - Michael Gould
Bernardo - Bernardo Kastlie
Nami - Kiana Pestonjee
Men in Dark Suits - Mark Flanagan, Kelly Shadburn
Young Samurai - Koji Kuninaga
Ninja - Sean Berry
Old Samurai - Master Richard Rabago
Martial Arts Teacher - Bruce Nguyen
Samurai Students - Katherine On
Kenneth Kim, Jae Lee
Cody Mau, Tiffany Le, Calvin Le
Samurai warrior - Master Ken Church

Special Guest Appearance - Briana Vigil

Kathleen Duey - Writer
Robert Gould - Creator/Photographer
Eugene Epstein - Digital Illustrator/Art Director/Story Board Artist
Mahsa Merat, Casting Director
Rakdy Khlok - Research and Costumes
Lara Gurin - Digital Composite Preparation
Jacob Dubizhansky - Digital Composite Preparation
Roman Gurinov - Image Masking
Carol Roland - Editing

Special thanks to:

Aya C. Ibarra - Japan Society of San Diego and Tijuana
Dave Tuites - Japan Society of San Diego Tijuana
Hiroko Johnson - San Diego State Curator, Historical Expert
Joyce Teague - Japanese American Historical Society of San Diego

Costuming and Props
Global Effects, Inc.
Kashu Sales International, Inc.
Aiya, Inc.
E-Bogu.com